PUFFIN BOOKS

A Little Princess

The next morning at breakfast, the girls could not stop whispering. When Sara came out of the kitchen carrying a large bowl of porridge, they fell silent.

'Sara, what happened?' Lottie whispered, as Sara served her.

'Sara!' Miss Minchin called sharply. She stood at the doorway. 'You are to serve the girls without talking!'

Miss Minchin turned towards the girls. 'Sara will be working here as a servant,' she explained. 'You are not to speak to her.'

The girls all nodded. Ermengarde stared at her bowl when Sara served her. She did not know what to do.

A Little Princess

A novelization by Diane Molleson

Based on the screenplay by
Richard La Gravenese and Elizabeth Chandler

Based on the book by
Frances Hodgson Burnett

PUFFIN BOOKS

PUFFIN BOOKS

Published by the Penguin Group
Penguin Books Ltd, 27 Wrights Lane, London w8 5tz, England
Penguin Books USA Inc., 375 Hudson Street, New York, New York 10014, USA
Penguin Books Australia Ltd, Ringwood, Victoria, Australia
Penguin Books Canada Ltd, 10 Alcorn Avenue, Toronto, Ontario, Canada m4v 3b2
Penguin Books (NZ) Ltd, 182–190 Wairau Road, Auckland 10, New Zealand

Penguin Books Ltd, Registered Offices: Harmondsworth, Middlesex, England

First published 1905
Published in Puffin Books 1961
Puffin Film and TV Tie-in edition first published 1996
3 5 7 9 10 8 6 4 2

Filmset in 13/15pt Baskerville

Made and printed in England by Clays Ltd, St Ives plc

CHAPTER ONE

India: August, 1914

Sara Crewe was not like many other ten-year-old girls. For a start, she lived in a mansion in India and every day she saw elephants, camels, gypsies in long veils, and men wearing turbans. Her father was a captain in the British army. Her mother, an American, had died when Sara was a baby.

Sara knew how to ride an elephant. She could also sing Indian folksongs and speak French. But, best of all, Sara used to make up the most magical stories, stories she sometimes believed were true. For Sara liked nothing better than daydreaming and musing.

One day Sara was sitting on the bank of the lake with Maya, her Indian nanny. While Laki, Maya's son was playing in the water with his baby elephant, Maya was telling Sara her favourite story. It was a very old Indian tale about a beautiful princess.

This was the story her nanny told Sara:

A long time ago, when the sun sat higher than it does today, there lived a beautiful princess in a land known as India. She was married to the handsome Prince Rama.

The princess whose name was Sita, lived with her husband in the enchanted forest because Prince Rama's jealous stepmother would not let them live in the kingdom. But the princess did not mind this. She loved her prince so much she would have lived with him anywhere.

One day, Princess Sita came upon a wounded gazelle lying in the woods. She begged Rama to go and help it.

However, the prince was afraid to leave Sita alone, for at the other end of the forest lived the evil ten-headed demon – Ravanna. Rama drew a circle in the ground.

'This is a magic circle,' he told Sita. 'As long as you stay inside it, no harm can come to you.'

Sita kissed her prince goodbye and promised she would remain inside the magic circle.

That night, the princess heard a horrible cry. Thinking her beloved Rama was in danger, the princess ran out of the magic circle. 'Rama, Rama!' she called out anxiously.

Soon the princess came upon an old beggar man. He looked so helpless that the kind-hearted princess wanted to help him. She had no food or money, so she took the long beaded bracelet off her wrist and gave it to him.

As soon as he had the bracelet in his hand, the beggar turned into the ten-headed demon – Ravanna! He caught hold of the princess and carried her off to his palace. You see, he wanted to make her his bride.

Far away, Rama was bending over the wounded gazelle. His hands moved over the animal's body, healing it. A monkey named Hanuman was watching Rama from the safety of a tree.

As soon as the gazelle was well again, Rama hurried away to rejoin his beloved princess. Imagine his horror when he found the magic circle empty.

Princess Sita was now a prisoner in Ravanna's tower. She spent the hours staring out of her small window.

One day a bird came and perched on her windowsill. The princess stroked the bird and whispered to it and it seemed to be listening to her.

Rama was staring sadly at the empty circle when the bird flew close to him and landed on his shoulder. It sang in his ear, telling him what had become of his princess. Then it flew up into the air and led him towards Ravanna's palace.

When the evil Ravanna spied the bird — and the prince — coming towards the tower, he fetched his bow and arrow. The first arrow he loosed flew straight and true, and hit the bird, which fell like a stone.

Ravanna then put ten more arrows into his bow and sent them all high into the air. The smoke from the arrows surrounded Prince Rama.

Although the prince did not know it, Hanuman, the monkey, was still following him. The monkey took a deep breath, then he blew the clouds of smoke away from the prince. But when the smoke cleared, the monkey saw that Rama was dead.

Then, suddenly, something wonderful happened. The gazelle that Rama had healed came wandering into the clearing. It lay down next to the fallen prince and brought him back to life.

Rama set out to rescue his bride without delay. This time the monkey led the way. As they drew near to the palace, a huge shadow fell over Rama: it was the shadow of the ten-headed demon. All his ten heads were enormous — and they were all very angry. How dare the prince approach his palace! Ravanna came towards the prince, ready to kill him.

Sita was watching from her window. She knew that the prince was about to die so she took the locket from round her neck, kissed it, and let it drop out of the window.

When the locket hit the ground, it burst open and a strange shape rose out of it. This shape then rose high in the sky.

Suddenly the sky grew dark with clouds and thunder rumbled overhead. A bolt of lightning struck Ravanna and killed him.

Sita leaned out of her tower window, smiling at the prince, as the sun came out above the clouds and shone all around.

Sara Crewe had heard that story over and over again, but she never tired of it.

'Did you ever know a real prince?' Sara asked Maya as she stroked the baby elephant's trunk.

'Yes . . . Laki's father,' her nanny answered.

'I mean real princes and princesses,' Sara asked.

'All women are princesses,' Maya said. 'It is our right.'

Sara smiled. Maybe she could be as much of a princess as the beautiful Princess Sita.

Chapter Two

Sara rode home from the lake on the back of the baby elephant. Laki, her nanny's son, led Sara and the elephant towards the mansion where Sara lived.

Sara and Laki looked at all the well-dressed men and women who were strolling about outside the house. Indian servants brought them cool drinks on sparkling silver trays.

The men and women were looking at Sara and Laki too. And they were not happy with what they saw. Sara was soaking wet from her swim in the lake, and she was wearing only her petticoat.

A group of British children crowded round Sara when the elephant stopped to take a drink from a water fountain. Laki helped Sara to climb down off the elephant. She smiled at him.

'Get that smelly animal out of here,' said a bossy twelve-year-old girl named Clara Pideson.

'I will not,' Sara answered. 'He's thirsty.' Sara did not like Clara at all.

'I wasn't talking about the elephant,' Clara said in a haughty voice.

Laki bowed his head in shame. Clara and some of the other children laughed, but Sara did not; she was very angry. She marched over to Clara and waved her hands above Clara's head. At the same time she chanted some words that made no sense.

'Stop that! What are you doing?' Clara demanded.

Sara stopped waving her hands and stared at Clara. 'I just put an ancient curse on you,' Sara answered her calmly. 'When you reach the age of twenty, all your hair will fall out, and every time you talk it will be backwards. So your name won't be Clara Pideson, it'll be Aralc Nosedip.'

'Aaahhhhh!' Clara screamed.

That evening, Sara was standing with her father in the middle of a wide meadow. They were both watching the sun setting over the high Himalayan mountains.

'I'll miss it here,' Sara's father said. 'India is the only place on earth that stirs the imagination.' He looked down at his daughter and shook his head. 'Not that you need any help in *that* department.'

Sara grinned back up at him. She loved being with her father.

'Aralc Nosedip, huh?' her father asked.

Sara shrugged. 'She asked for it.'

Captain Andrew Crewe smiled and put his arm round Sara.

'I wish the summer would never end,' she said sadly.

Captain Crewe knelt down in front of his daughter. 'It'll be all right, sweetheart. You're going to love America.'

'But it's so far away,' Sara said. 'Why can't I go to school in England? At least we'd be closer to each other.'

'England's no place for a young girl until this war is over.' Her father's voice was firm. 'Besides, you'll be going to the same school your mother went to when she was your age. In a city called New York.'

Sara laid her head on her father's shoulder. 'New York,' she said. 'What a silly name.'

CHAPTER THREE

On the night before they set sail for America, Sara slept soundly in her own pretty bedroom. When her father came in to kiss her good night, she woke up.

'Big day tomorrow. Almost like going on an adventure, isn't it?' Captain Crewe said. He tried to sound cheerful, but Sara could tell that he was feeling sad. 'I promise we'll spend every minute together until we reach New York,' her father added.

Sara looked pleased. She smiled even more when she saw that he had put a package, wrapped in fancy paper, on her bed.

Sara sat up to open her present. '*The Ramayana*!' Sara exclaimed in delight. *The Ramayana* was a classic Indian epic and Sara's favourite story about the princess was in it.

'In there is every story I ever told you,' her father said.

'And now I can tell them to myself, as if you were really there. Except I'll never be able to do all those voices as well as you. Especially the monsters.'

Captain Crewe wrinkled his nose. 'Oh,' he said, sounding as if he had a cold. 'The monsters have this sort of squeaky, nasal quality.'

Sara wrinkled her nose too. She tried to speak in the same squeaky voice as her father. 'Like this?'

'A bit more wrinkled,' her father replied.

'Oh cursed prince, thou hast drawn thy last breath,' Sara said, pretending she had a stuffy nose.

Her father chuckled. 'Perfect. You'll do just fine,' he said.

'Daddy,' Sara said. She sat up a little straighter in her bed. 'Maya told me all girls are princesses.'

'Maya is a very wise woman,' her father answered, smiling. 'I believe you are, and always will be, my little princess,' he added softly.

The following day, travellers, merchants, servants and porters were all crowding together on the dock. Captain Crewe made sure that the porter had loaded their trunks safely on to the big ship. Sara sat on the shore, watching the dock scene with wide eyes. It was so hot, she welcomed the cool breeze which she suddenly felt on her neck.

Sara turned around and saw that an Indian man was staring at her. A monkey was sitting on the man's shoulder. Sara stared back at the man until some other people passed in front of him. When these people had walked on, Sara saw that the man had gone.

Sara did not know it at the time, but the man's name was Ram Dass. She would see him again in New York.

At that moment the ship's horn let out a loud blast. Everyone scrambled aboard. Sara and her father were on their way to America.

That evening, on board the ship, Sara's father gave her a beautiful gold locket. 'I gave this to your mother on our wedding day,' Captain Crewe explained. 'I want you to have it.'

Sara gazed up at her father; she looked and felt as if she was on the point of bursting into tears. Slowly she undid the clasp and opened the locket.

Inside were two pictures. One was of her father; Sara thought he looked just like Prince Rama. The other was of her mother, who looked like the Princess Sita in Sara's dreams.

'She was so beautiful,' Sara said proudly.

Captain Crewe gently took the locket and fastened it round Sara's neck.

Several weeks later, the ship they were on glided by the Statue of Liberty. Sara and her father had arrived in New York.

CHAPTER FOUR

New York: 1914

A horse-drawn carriage sped along the bustling city streets. It turned into a tree-lined square and stopped in front of a large, brownstone house. Captain Crewe helped Sara from the carriage and paid the driver.

Sara walked slowly up the brownstone steps until she came to the gold plaque near the front door. It said:

MISS MINCHIN'S SEMINARY
FOR GIRLS
Established 1856

Sara took a deep breath before she rang the doorbell. On the second floor of the house, a black servant-girl pushed open a window and looked out. Sara looked back up at her.

Amelia Minchin, the sister of the school's headmistress, opened the front door to them. Amelia was a plump, cheerful woman. 'Hello! You must be Captain Crewe,' she said, eyeing the handsome, well-dressed captain. 'Please come in!'

Sara and her father followed Amelia into a large, cold hallway. 'My sister will be down presently,' she told the captain. 'We were just preparing the young lady's room. Your beautiful things arrived this morning,' she added, staring at Sara.

'Thank you . . .' Captain Crewe answered. His voice faded away and his eyebrows rose. Amelia had quite forgotten to tell him her name.

'Oh! Heavens! Amelia . . . Amelia Minchin,' Amelia said, smiling as she shook Captain Crewe's hand once more.

Sara smiled. Amelia Minchin seemed all right. Maybe this cold-looking school wouldn't be so bad after all.

The moment Sara met the other Miss Minchin, she did not feel so happy any more. The other Miss Minchin was thin and severe. She talked, non-stop, about school rules. And she never smiled.

'Classes begin promptly at eight o'clock,' Miss Minchin told Sara and her father as she led them through the parlour. 'We cover all subjects – literature, mathematics, science and, of course, French and Latin.'

'Oh, Sara speaks fluent . . .' Captain Crewe began.

Miss Minchin didn't give him a chance to finish. 'Lunch is served at one thirty, after which we take our daily walk,' she said as she led Sara and her father along a dreary corridor. 'Study hall is from four thirty to six thirty, followed by a light supper,' she went on.

Sara wondered if Miss Minchin ever stopped talking.

'Before bedtime we read from one of the great classics – something the children always look forward to,' Miss Minchin added.

Sara frowned. Miss Minchin's Seminary did not sound like a whole lot of fun.

Miss Minchin suddenly opened one of the doors leading out of the hall. Sara and her father followed her into a big classroom. A large group of girls all turned to see the new arrivals. The girls ranged in age from six to twelve. Their French teacher, Monsieur DuFarge, was asleep at his desk.

Miss Minchin coughed loudly so that the teacher woke up with a start.

'Girls, I would like you to say hello to our new arrival – Miss Sara Crewe.'

'Hello, Sara,' the girls said slowly.

'You must tell them about your exciting life in India,' Miss Minchin said to Sara in a loud whisper. Then she turned to Sara's father. 'No doubt she'll be our most popular student in no time,' she added.

Sara looked very embarrassed. All the girls had heard Miss Minchin's words. One of them, Lavinia, gave Sara a scowl. Lavinia, at the age of twelve, thought *she* was the most popular girl in the school. She did not want anyone taking her place, especially not a ten-year-old.

Miss Minchin turned her back on the schoolgirls and led Sara and her father to the window. It was time for her to tell them the important school rules. Number One – The Communication Rule. In order to learn concentration, the girls were not allowed to talk or look at or write to one another except during their free time.

Out of the corner of her eye, Sara saw Lavinia reach out and grab the pigtail of a plump girl in front of her. Lavinia dipped the pigtail into her inkwell.

'The Order Rule,' Miss Minchin continued, 'teaches the girls to attend to their rooms. The Tidiness Rule helps them in caring for their personal appearance.'

Sara sighed.

'Also, I'm afraid that jewellery and other such finery are not allowed.' Miss Minchin's voice was firm. She looked pointedly at Sara's locket.

Sara's hand flew to her neck. 'Well, could I wear it in my room, during my free time?' she asked politely but firmly.

The other students gasped. No one dared to stand up to Miss Minchin.

'Well, if you absolutely insist,' Miss Minchin replied icily. She looked at Sara's father for help.

'I do,' Sara said.

Captain Crewe grinned at his daughter. It was clear whose side he was on.

Miss Minchin looked very angry. However, she forced a smile for Captain Crewe's sake. But, from that moment on, Miss Minchin took a strong dislike to her new pupil.

CHAPTER FIVE

Miss Minchin coughed softly. She had come to the end of her tour, showing Sara and her father the school grounds. They stood in front of her in the school's small quadrangle.

'Now I come to the part I find most delicate,' she said. '. . . Payment.'

'Oh yes,' Captain Crewe answered. 'My solicitor, Mr Barrow, has instructions to send payments to you every month.' He handed Miss Minchin the lawyer's business card. 'Whatever Sara needs, you just let Mr Barrow know.'

Miss Minchin looked very satisfied. She led the way up to Sara's room with a look of pride on her face.

Sara had the prettiest room in the school – her father had made sure of that. The room had windows at each corner and a large fireplace. Sara's toys and books had arrived, so had her fine clothes. Her father always made sure that Sara had the best of everything.

Miss Minchin left Sara and her father alone so that they could say their goodbyes. They did not have much time before he would have to leave.

Captain Crewe sat down on a chair and pulled his daughter onto his lap. 'We'll write each other every day,' he said as he gave her a big hug.

Sara tried to smile.

'You know,' Captain Crewe began. His eyes twinkled. 'I think I saw something . . . on that chair over there.'

Sara looked across the room and saw a doll's foot sticking out behind a chair. She walked slowly across the room and picked up the beautiful new doll.

'She came all the way from France to be with you,' Mr Crewe explained. 'Her name is Emily.'

Sara nodded sadly. Her father saw at once that the new doll would never make up for him being away. He walked over to his daughter and knelt beside her.

'You know,' Mr Crewe said softly, 'dolls make

the very best friends. Just because they can't speak, it doesn't mean they don't listen. Did you know, when we leave them alone, they come to life?'

Sara looked up and shook her head. Her blue eyes brightened as the pain inside her lessened just a little.

'Yes,' her father said. 'Before we walk in and catch them, they return to their places, quick as lightning.'

'Why don't they come to life in front of us, so we can see?' Sara asked.

'Because it's magic,' her father replied. 'Magic has to be believed. That's the only way it's real.'

Sara looked at her new doll proudly.

Her father reached out and stroked his daughter's hair. 'Whenever you miss me terribly,' he began, 'just tell Emily. She'll get the message to me, wherever I am.' His voice shook. 'And then I'll send one back right away, so that when you hug her, you'll really be getting a hug from me.'

Sara was comforted by this thought, but her father looked heartbroken. He bowed his head so that Sara wouldn't see the tears in his eyes.

Sara had never seen her father act in this way before. She took his hand gently. 'It's all right, Daddy. I'm going to be fine.'

Mr Crewe gazed at Sara with a look of pride on his face. 'I know,' he said softly.

When twilight came, Mr Crewe walked to his carriage. Then he turned and looked up at Sara. She was waving to him from her bedroom window.

'Goodbye, Princess,' he called softly to her.

Sara held Emily tightly. Together they watched her father's carriage pull away from the kerb.

Chapter Six

The following morning, the schoolgirls at Miss Minchin's Seminary were all sitting at the large breakfast table and talking about Sara.

'Did you see all her toys?' asked six-year-old Ruth.

'Her father grows crackers or something. They're very rich,' said an eight-year-old named Jane.

'Her father is British. I heard he's best friends with the King and Queen,' added Betsy, who was ten.

Lavinia was growing more and more angry. Why was everyone talking about the new girl? 'Hah!' she said loudly. 'I heard he was thrown out of India because people died eating his poisoned crackers.'

'Really?' Gertrude replied. 'I once had an aunt who died from eating poisoned string beans.'

'Oh, who cares about her!' Lavinia said rudely.

Sara rushed out of her bedroom, still tying her hair-ribbon. She knew she was late for breakfast. She closed the door to her room then stopped. Maybe she could catch Emily moving. She peeked back in through the keyhole.

Emily was sitting quietly in her chair, exactly as Sara had left her. 'Boy, she's fast,' Sara murmured.

She rushed down the stairs. Photographs of former classes were hung on the wall opposite the banister. Sara stopped and looked at them; she was searching through all the faces in all the pictures until she found her mother's.

'Sara!' Miss Minchin called out. She was standing at the bottom of the stairs. 'We are not accustomed to delaying breakfast for one student.'

'I'm sorry, Miss Minchin,' Sara said as she went down the last few stairs. 'But I found —'

'You're not the only child here, Sara. You must remember that,' Miss Minchin's voice was cold.

Soon after breakfast, Sara went to her maths class. She sat down at the back of the room.

'Seven times six is forty-two,' said Betsy.

'Seven times seven is forty-nine,' said Gertrude.

'Seven times eight is . . . fifty-eight. No, no . . . fifty-four. No, wait . . .' Ermengarde said, flustered. She burned bright red.

Sara felt sorry for Ermengarde: Ermengarde was the one Lavinia always picked on. Just yesterday, it was Ermengarde's hair that Lavinia had dipped in the inkwell.

'I'm sorry, Miss Minchin. I studied for hours last night. Honest, I did,' Ermengarde said.

Miss Minchin gave Ermengarde a cold stare. 'I find that very hard to believe. I imagine your father will as well.'

'Oh, please don't tell him, Miss Minchin.' Ermengarde sounded horrified.

'Lavinia, you may continue,' Miss Minchin said, ignoring poor Ermengarde.

Lavinia smirked. 'Seven times eight is fifty-six.'

Later that day, the girls played in groups in the school quadrangle. Sara sat alone reading *The Ramayana*. Ermengarde, also alone, whispered the times tables to herself.

Sara looked up from her reading. Lavinia and her hanger-on, Jesse, were giggling at her. Sara did her best to ignore them.

Suddenly Amelia appeared at the door. 'Sara! Miss Minchin would like to see you in your room right away.'

Sara looked up in surprise. Lavinia and Jesse were giggling more loudly than ever. They must have something to do with this, Sara thought to herself.

Sara slowly went up to her room. What she saw when she got there made her stop and gasp: her beautiful clothes and toys had been scattered all over the floor.

Miss Minchin was standing in the middle of the mess. She was trying on one of Sara's silk capes in front of the mirror. Sara stood and watched her, unsure what to do or say. 'Miss Minchin?' she said finally in a small, timid voice.

Miss Minchin whirled around. She had certainly not known that Sara was watching her and she was ashamed that she had been caught trying on the girl's clothes. That made her even angrier.

'This room is a disgrace! I want it picked up immediately. Is that clear?' Miss Minchin said. She threw Sara's cape on the chair and stormed out of the room.

CHAPTER SEVEN

It was late in the afternoon by the time Sara had finished straightening up her room. She sat in her windowseat with Emily, writing a letter to her father.

Dear Daddy,
... Things are fine, except that everybody here seems to be mad at me ... in the same way Clara back home was always mad. I don't see how you can go from one end of the world to the other and still meet the same people ...

Sara stopped writing and looked up. Then she noticed two men in the street below. They were standing in front of the brownstone house, next to the school. One was in a wheelchair and the

26

other was a young soldier in uniform. As they tearfully hugged each other goodbye, Sara remembered the scene when she had had to say goodbye to her own father. A teardrop ran down her cheek and fell on her letter.

Sara did not know how long she had been crying when she suddenly heard loud noises coming from outside her room. Someone was having a tantrum − and not a little one either, but a full-scale one, with lots of shrieking and kicking.

'Lottie, you mustn't get so upset. Here, play with your music-box,' Amelia was saying.

Lottie only howled more loudly.

'Oh, you wicked child. I'll shake you, I will.' Amelia sounded desperate. 'Please stop screaming. How about a cookie? Would you like that?'

Amelia rushed downstairs to the kitchen to find a biscuit. A second later, Sara opened her bedroom door. She stood in the doorway for a moment, calmly watching the little girl who was still screaming. 'You know,' Sara said finally, 'it's very hard to study with you carrying on like this.'

'I want my mama!' Lottie wailed.

'You'll see her soon,' Sara said, raising her voice, above the shrieks.

27

'No, I won't! She's dead. I won't ever see her again!'

Sara walked over to Lottie. 'Well, I don't have a mother either.'

Lottie stopped screaming. Her eyes widened and she looked interested. 'You don't? Where is she?'

'In heaven,' Sara answered simply. 'But that doesn't mean I can't talk to her. I tell her everything, and I know she hears me.'

'How?' Lottie asked. By now she'd stopped kicking and screaming altogether.

'Because that's what angels do.'

'Your mama's an angel?' Lottie sounded delighted by this.

Sara knelt down beside the little girl. 'Of course. And so is yours,' she answered. 'With wings of silk and a crown of golden roses.'

Lottie's eyes grew wider as Sara kept talking, making up a wonderful story as she went along.

Sara told Lottie that their mothers were living together in a castle that was surrounded by hundreds of flowers – and filled with music.

Further down the hall, Ermengarde opened her door a little so that she could hear Sara's story. The servant girl, Becky, peeked over the top stair. She didn't want to miss a word.

Suddenly Becky's shoe squeaked on one of the stairs. Sara turned around, in time to see Becky jumping up and rushing towards the attic door like a frightened mouse.

'Oh, wait,' Sara called after her. But Becky had disappeared up the attic staircase.

'That's Becky,' Lottie tried to explain to Sara. 'We're not allowed to talk to her.'

'Why not?' Sara asked wonderingly.

'She's a servant girl – and she has dark skin.'

'*So*?' Sara asked sharply.

'Well, doesn't that mean something?' Lottie asked. She looked rather confused.

Sara was curious about Becky. So, later that afternoon, she climbed the narrow attic staircase and pushed open the door to Becky's room.

Becky was sitting on her narrow cot in the dark, bare room. She had not heard Sara come in and she was busy taking off a pair of old shoes that looked much too small for her. Sara was shocked to see how swollen and blistered Becky's feet were.

Suddenly a board creaked under Sara's foot. Becky whirled around and jumped to her feet.

'Oh, I'm sorry. I didn't mean . . .' Sara stammered. For once she couldn't think of anything to say.

'Is there anything I can do for you, Miss? I just came up to change my shoes.'

'No, nothing,' Sara replied.

'Well, then. Begging your pardon, but we'll both be in trouble if you stay,' Becky said. She was watching Sara guardedly.

Sara nodded and left the room.

The following day, Becky found a parcel with a note on her cot. She opened the note and read:

> *Dear Becky,*
> *I'm sorry. Hope we can still be friends.*
> *Sara*

Inside the box was a pair of furry slippers. Becky gratefully slid them on her tired feet.

CHAPTER EIGHT

In the evenings, the girls at Miss Minchin's school gathered in the dining-room for their nightly reading hour. Tonight, they were taking it in turns to read from a dull novel. Miss Minchin and Amelia sat in their chairs, listening sleepily.

Ermengarde read the boring story without any expression in her voice. The other girls fell asleep or sat and fidgeted in their chairs. How they hated these evenings! Only Sara appeared to be listening. The story made her angry: how could the heroine in the book marry a man against her will?

When it was her turn to read, Sara decided to change the ending. She had Charlotte, the heroine, run away from home with her lover,

Pierre. The two set sail for a tropical island and were captured by a band of pirates!

When they heard Sara's new ending to the novel, the girls began to stir in their chairs. They nudged one another awake and listened to every word.

Miss Minchin began to sense that something was wrong. She snatched the book from Sara and started thumbing through it. Sara calmly went on with her version of the story: 'Charlotte and Pierre threw themselves overboard – and were rescued by a band of mermaids.'

The girls gasped in delight.

Miss Minchin threw the book down. 'Stop!' she shouted at Sara. 'What do you think you're doing?'

'I imagined a different ending,' Sara explained.

'You imagined it,' Miss Minchin said scornfully.

Sara nodded. 'Don't you ever do that, Miss Minchin? Believe in something, just to make it seem real?'

'I suppose that's rather easy for a child who has everything,' Miss Minchin replied tartly.

Sara looked hurt.

'From now on, there will be no more "make-believe" during reading hour, or at any other time, in this school. Is that understood?' Miss Minchin's voice was firm. Then she dismissed them.

The girls plodded up the stairs to their bedrooms. They were sorry that they hadn't been allowed to hear Sara's story through to the end. Sara, Ermengarde, Betsy and Gertrude were the last to make their way up the stairs.

'I've never heard a story like that in my whole life!' Betsy exclaimed.

'You must know a lot more good stories like that,' Ermengarde added.

'I have an idea,' Betsy said to Sara. Her eyes twinkled. 'After Minchin goes to bed, we'll sneak into your room and you can show us what a real story is.'

'Oh, yes, yes!' Ermengarde and Betsy said at once.

'Well,' Sara answered, 'maybe if it's just you three.'

That night, many more girls than three crowded into Sara's room to listen to the story of Princess Sita. Each night Sara told them a new chapter.

Before long, Sara could write to her father with some good news. She had now made some new friends – Ermengarde, Lottie, Betsy and Gertrude. Best of all, she had a secret friend: Becky. In a way, Sara felt closer to Becky than she did to any of the other girls. Though she missed her father terribly, she was beginning to like Miss Minchin's Seminary a little better.

Chapter Nine

Far away, on a battlefield, somewhere in Europe, Captain Crewe read his daughter's latest letter with tears in his eyes. He wished he could be with her.

'Captain!' a soldier called out, interrupting Crewe's daydream. 'Colonel Harding just called. The enemy line is advancing. Our orders are to retreat immediately.'

Captain Crewe looked around. What few troops were left in his sector looked scared and numb. 'Start moving out,' he said.

Captain Crewe picked up his kitbag and set off in the footsteps of his men. Suddenly he heard the sound of someone groaning at his feet. He knelt down at the side of the young soldier lying wounded on the ground. The young man was shaking with fever.

'Hey, we need a medic here!' Captain Crewe shouted, but the others had already disappeared. The captain took off his jacket and wrapped it round the young soldier. Then he lifted the wounded man on to his shoulder and set out as quickly as he could. He could hear the engines of German war planes flying overhead.

As the sound of the planes grew closer, Captain Crewe froze. Then, recovering himself, he quickly lowered the soldier and pulled the two of them against the shelter of the trench wall.

The war planes dropped canisters of gas on the deserted battlefield. Soon clouds of yellow smoke were moving towards Crewe and the young soldier. Captain Crewe began to choke. He tied a handkerchief over the young soldier's face, then he climbed out of the trench and tried to pull the soldier out after him. But the poisonous gas soon overpowered them both.

Slowly Captain Crewe lost consciousness. The young soldier slid back into the trench, but Crewe's body was still lying on the open ground.

CHAPTER TEN

At Miss Minchin's Seminary, the dining-room had been decorated for a birthday party. A big cake with twelve candles occupied the place of honour in the middle of the table. All the girls crowded round Sara as she blew out her candles and began to cut the cake. Miss Minchin and Amelia were watching from the doorway.

'I want a big piece!' Lottie reminded Sara.

'Oh, hush up, Lottie,' Lavinia said rudely. 'I'm sure *Princess* Sara will give everyone a fair share. Right, Princess?' she added, turning to Sara.

Lottie gave Sara a sheepish look. 'I told her that's what you were,' she explained.

'Not just me,' Sara said. 'All girls are princesses. Even snotty, two-faced bullies like you, Lavinia.'

Lavinia glared at Sara, but the other girls giggled. Miss Minchin frowned and was on the point of scolding Sara when the doorbell rang. Before she went to answer the door, Miss Minchin gave Sara a disapproving look.

Mr Barrow, Captain Crewe's lawyer, was standing at the door. 'May I speak with you in private?' he asked Miss Minchin.

'Yes, of course. Right this way,' Miss Minchin said as she led the lawyer into her office.

'Before you begin, Mr Barrow, may I just say, Sara is quite the favourite around here,' Miss Minchin said. 'We went to great expense to make this a special birthday. I'm afraid your cheque to us this month will be rather large.'

'There will be no more cheques, Miss Minchin,' the lawyer replied. The expression on his face was sombre.

'Excuse me?' Miss Minchin asked. She could not believe her ears.

The lawyer stepped into her office and closed the door.

While Miss Minchin was talking to the lawyer, the party in the dining-room grew merrier and merrier. The older girls were playing a game with Sara. They put a blindfold over her eyes and she had to try to catch and name them. Amelia and Ermengarde were playing a jazzy tune on the piano. Soon they were all swinging their hips and tapping their feet to the music.

Miss Minchin appeared at the doorway and watched the scene in silence for some moments. Then she suddenly stormed over to the piano and slammed the lid down over the keys.

Amelia and the girls fell silent. They had never seen Miss Minchin look so angry.

Miss Minchin tore off Sara's blindfold. 'This party is over,' she announced. 'I want everyone to go to their rooms.'

'But, we . . .' Sara began.

'Sara,' Miss Minchin said in her coldest voice, 'you will stay behind. I have something to tell you.'

The other girls scrambled out of the door; they were all frightened by Miss Minchin's tone of voice.

'Amelia, go to Sara's room and find a simple black dress,' Miss Minchin said next.

'But —' Amelia protested.

'Do as I say!' Miss Minchin snapped. As Amelia hurried away, Miss Minchin turned back to Sara.

'Why will I need a black dress?' Sara asked, puzzled.

'I'm afraid I have some bad news, Sara,' Miss Minchin began. 'Your father has . . .' She paused and took a deep breath. 'Your father has died. He was killed in battle, several weeks ago.'

Sara turned pale. She sat down in the nearest chair and stared out of the window.

Miss Minchin continued. 'The war left his company without any money. You are now penniless. And you have no relatives who can take care of you.'

Sara went on looking out of the window without moving. She didn't say a word.

'What are you staring at?' Miss Minchin snapped. She was a little scared of Sara. 'Don't you understand what I am saying? You are alone in the world, unless I decide to keep you here!'

Neither Sara nor Miss Minchin saw Becky hiding behind the door. The little servant-girl had heard every word and she felt frightened and sorry for Sara. Outside, a storm was brewing and thunder rumbled overhead.

'Your clothes, your toys, everything now belongs to me. Though they will hardly make up for the money I spent on your party,' Miss Minchin continued.

Rain began to pelt against the window-pane. Sara did not look up.

Miss Minchin cleared her throat. 'From now on, you must earn your room and board here.'

Sara was making her feel more and more nervous. Why didn't the child say something?

'You will be moved to the attic with Becky and work as a servant – cleaning, running errands and helping Mabel in the kitchen,' Miss Minchin finished.

Chapter Eleven

That evening, Miss Minchin led Sara to her attic room in the tower. The light from Miss Minchin's candle flickered on the dirty walls.

Sara was now wearing a simple black dress. In her arms she was clutching Emily and her bedclothes. She followed Miss Minchin slowly up the narrow staircase.

'If you don't do as you are told, you'll be thrown out,' Miss Minchin reminded Sara. Sara's eyes widened. She did not want to be left, alone and homeless, in New York City.

Miss Minchin opened the door to Sara's attic room which was opposite Becky's. The walls were made out of rotting wooden planks. Cobwebs hung in every corner. Water leaked in through the skylight in the low, slanting roof.

'You will report to Mabel in the kitchen at five a.m.' Miss Minchin said. As she turned to go, she saw that Sara was carrying a book and her locket inside a blanket.

Miss Minchin took the locket and glared at her. 'I could have you arrested for taking this,' she said. 'I expect you to remember, Sara Crewe . . . you're not a princess any longer,' she added as she left the room.

Sara sat, alone, in the dark. The walls of her room creaked. The wind made the shutters outside her small window bang, and rain dripped from the skylight on to the floor.

Sara trembled. She took a piece of coal from the fireplace and drew a big circle on the floor with it. Then she curled up inside the circle and cried and cried. 'Daddy . . . Daddy,' she called.

Chapter Twelve

The next morning at breakfast, the girls could not stop whispering. When Sara came out of the kitchen carrying a large bowl of porridge, they fell silent.

'Sara, what happened?' Lottie whispered, as Sara served her.

'Sara!' Miss Minchin called sharply. She was standing in the doorway. 'You are to serve the girls without talking!'

Miss Minchin turned towards the girls. 'Sara will be working here as a servant,' she explained. 'You are not to speak to her.'

The girls all nodded. Ermengarde sat and stared down at her bowl when Sara served her; she did not know what to do.

*

~♥~

'Morning, Miss Amelia,' said Francis, the milk-man, as he came into the kitchen. Francis liked Amelia.

'Oh, good morning Francis,' Amelia answered, patting her hair with one hand.

Sara held a tray of breakfast dishes while she watched them. Francis put the milk bottles on the kitchen table and complimented Amelia on how well she was looking. Amelia flushed with pleasure.

Mabel, the cook, was watching Sara and she saw that the girl wasn't doing anything. 'Hurry up and rinse those dishes!' she snapped. Sara rushed to obey her.

For Sara, each day was drearier than the last: she woke up early to serve breakfast, wash the dishes, mop the floors and run errands. Miss Minchin and Mabel kept after her all the time. They loved having someone to boss around, especially someone who had once had everything.

Sara's hands grew red and blistered. Her few dresses became worn and frayed and her shoes had holes in them.

One day, while Sara was out running errands, a gust of wind lifted her thin shawl clean off her shoulders and with a cry, she ran after it. The shawl landed in the square outside the school – right at a man's feet.

Sara looked at the man in surprise. He was Indian, and she knew she had seen him before. He was the man who had stared at her on the docks. The man was staring at her again as she picked up her shawl.

Suddenly they both heard someone cry out. Sara turned to see what was happening. As she watched, two soldiers in uniform were delivering a telegram to Mr Randolph, the old man in the wheelchair who lived next door to the school.

Mr Randolph read the telegram, then he bowed his head and wept. 'Not my son,' he moaned. 'Please, not John.'

The Indian man left Sara and went across to put his hand on Mr Randolph's shoulder. The Indian man must live next door, too, Sara thought to herself.

Sara remembered having watched Mr Randolph say goodbye to his son. It seemed so long ago now. The young man must have been killed, just like her own father.

'Sara!' Miss Minchin called out from the doorway. Sara jumped and hurried back to school.

*

46

That evening, Sara was sitting on a crate in her room, looking out of the window. A wooden plank in the wall suddenly creaked even more loudly than usual. Sara turned in time to see Becky squeezing through a small gap between the planks.

'Sara,' Becky said gently, 'why don't you tell your stories any more?'

'Stories . . .' Sara replied softly.

'They might make you feel better,' Becky urged her friend.

Sara shook her head. 'They're just make-believe. They don't mean anything.'

'They've always meant something to me,' Becky insisted. 'There were days I thought I'd die till I heard you talk about the magic.'

Sara stared out of the window. 'There is no magic, Becky.'

Becky looked heartbroken to see Sara like this. She turned and went silently back to her own attic room.

Sara sat alone in the dark and whispered, 'Daddy, can you hear me? I'm so scared.' She picked Emily up off the floor. 'Can he hear me, Emily?'

Emily stayed still and unmoving. 'Oh, you're nothing but a doll!' Sara cried out and she threw Emily back onto the floor.

On the other side of the wall, Becky lay awake for a long time. She could hear Sara crying until long into the night.

CHAPTER THIRTEEN

The girls at Miss Minchin's school paired up in the school quadrangle for their daily walk. Sara was left raking leaves in the corner. Timidly, Lottie broke away from her companions and ran to Sara.

'Sara, are you still a princess?' Lottie asked her friend.

This was the first time any of the girls had spoken to Sara since her birthday party. She turned in surprise.

'Get back in line, Lottie,' she said softly. 'We'll both be in trouble.' She did not tell Lottie that she no longer believed in princesses.

'Lottie!' Miss Minchin called as she stepped through the door, ready to take the girls for their walk. Lottie hurried back to her place in

49

the crocodile. As they set off, Ermengarde glanced back at Sara, and Sara looked up at her and smiled. Because Miss Minchin was watching them all closely, Ermengarde was too afraid to smile back.

Sara felt hurt. She went back to her raking, while Ermengarde lowered her head in shame and followed the group out.

One cold winter's evening Sara was wandering through New York's busy meat market. The smell of all the food made her feel faint with hunger; she had had no supper. Quickly, she did the shopping that Mabel had ordered her to get, then hurried back to school.

On the way home, she began to feel very tired. The parcels felt as heavy as lead in her arms. She put them down and leant against a shop window to rest.

A well-dressed boy was walking along the street with his mother. The boy glanced at Sara, then he pressed a coin into her hand. 'Here, little girl,' he said.

Sara looked up in shock. Then, slowly, she turned to look at her reflection in the shop window. No wonder the boy had given her money: her clothes looked like rags and her face was pale and pinched. She looked just like one of New York's many street beggars.

Sara kept on staring. She was looking into the window of a baker's shop. Cakes, pies, fresh bread and buns were piled up in the shop window. Sara walked inside.

A few moment later, Sara was sitting on the steps outside the bakery. She took the steaming-hot bun out of its bag and lifted it to her mouth. But then she noticed something that stopped her from taking the first bite.

A tired beggar woman was walking along the street, holding a baby in one arm and carrying a basket of yellow roses in the other. Sara watched as the woman tried in vain to sell the roses to the passers-by. No one would buy any from her.

Sara walked slowly up to the woman and offered the hot bun to the baby. The woman gazed at Sara with a look of surprise; she did not expect such kindness from someone who looked just as poor as she did.

'Wait!' she called, as Sara turned away. Then the woman handed her a yellow rose out of her basket. 'For the princess . . .' she said, smiling.

Sara could only smile back: she was too moved to answer. She picked up her parcels and hurried back to Miss Minchin's. As she passed Mr Randolph's house, she saw a black bow pinned to his front door. The old man was sitting by the fireplace, his head bowed. Sara gently laid her yellow rose on his doorstep.

That evening, the moonlight came flooding into Sara's attic room. She lay on her cot, staring at a mouse. The mouse stared back at Sara, twitching its whiskers.

'What is it, little mouse? Are you a prisoner, too?' Sara asked it.

It was so cold in the room, Sara could see the cloud that her breath made, and she shivered under her thin blanket.

On the other side of the wall, Becky was shivering, too. She thought for a long moment, then she knocked on the wall. 'Sara, are you awake?' she called out.

'Yes,' Sara replied.

'Is it ever this cold where you come from?' Becky wanted to know.

'No,' Sara said softly.

'Tell me, Sara. Tell me again about India,' Becky pleaded.

Sara sighed. 'Well, the air is so hot there, you can almost taste it.'

Becky smiled. This was the first time Sara had told her a story since her father's death. 'I bet it tastes like coconuts,' she mused.

'No,' Sara said, thinking. 'The air smells more like spices – curry and saffron . . .'

Sara drifted off to sleep, dreaming about India. When she woke up, moonlight was still pouring through her window. She sat up – to find that her bed was covered with yellow rose-petals! Outside, she could hear a man's voice; he was singing an Indian folksong – the same folksong that she used to sing in India.

Sara climbed out of bed and looked out through the window. In the street a man in a turban was singing softly into the night – the same man who stared at Sara whenever he chanced to meet her.

Sara lifted her arms above her head and began to dance round the room. She stopped dancing when the song ended, and now she felt strangely at peace. For the first time since her father had died, she felt like a princess again.

CHAPTER FOURTEEN

The following morning, Sara saw the Indian man again, outside in the street. A monkey was perched on his shoulder.

'Hanuman,' Sara said, greeting them. 'Hanuman' was the name of the monkey in *The Ramayana*.

The Indian man smiled to discover that Sara knew something about India. He greeted her in his native language. This time, it was Sara who grinned: she understood him perfectly.

Just then, the school's back door was flung open. Miss Minchin stood in the doorway, with the school's chimney sweep beside her.

'You can forget being paid this week,' Miss Minchin told the sweep angrily. 'I told you I don't want the slightest bit of dirt in this house. Just look at my boot, it's filthy.'

'But . . .' the poor sweep protested. He looked thin and tired, and he was covered in soot.

'Out, out!' Miss Minchin shouted.

The sweep trudged away down the street. Before he left, he dumped his big bags of soot by the rubbish bin that stood near Sara.

Sara looked at the bags of soot thoughtfully. They gave her an idea.

Later that day, Sara carried a bag of soot up to her room. Leaning out of her window, she carefully passed the bag to Becky, who was perched on the roof.

Then Sara joined Becky on the roof. Together, they tipped the bag over above the chimney. A few specks of soot trickled down to the fireplace in Miss Minchin's study.

Miss Minchin was sitting at her desk, correcting essays. When she heard bits of soot falling down the chimney, she stopped her work and bent down at the fireplace to take a look upwards, to see what was causing the soot to fall.

'Whoosh!!' The whole load of soot cascaded down the chimney and covered Miss Minchin from head to foot in black soot. 'Aahhh!!' she screamed.

*

That evening, at dinner, everyone noticed that Miss Minchin was looking a little strange; she had scrubbed and scrubbed her face with soap and water. Even so, it still looked grey from all the soot, except for two circles round her eyes where her glasses had protected her.

The schoolgirls could not help giggling when they saw her. Ermengarde watched Sara and Becky exchange secret smiles. Something told her that they were behind all this, and she felt left out.

Later that evening, Ermengarde climbed the attic stairs and pushed open Sara's door.

'Is this where you live?' she asked in a voice choked with emotion.

Sara looked up in surprise at seeing her friend. 'You shouldn't be here, Ermengarde,' was all she said.

Ermengarde felt tears in her eyes. 'Oh, Sara, why don't you like me any more? Did I do something wrong?'

Sara looked stunned. 'No, of course not. I just didn't think you wanted me as a friend, now that . . . now that things are different.'

'Oh Sara, no,' Ermengarde protested. 'I couldn't get along without you.'

Sara looked touched. 'I'm sorry, Ermengarde. I should've known you wouldn't be like the others.'

The two girls smiled at each other.

Suddenly, they both heard someone knocking on the bedroom wall. Ermengarde jumped. 'What's that?' she asked.

Sara crossed over to the wall. 'One knock means I'm here,' she explained to Ermengarde as she rapped on the wall with her knuckles. 'Two knocks means all is well. Three knocks means the demon Minchinweed is asleep.'

'Oh Sara, it all sounds so adventurous,' Ermengarde said after Becky wormed her way through the hole in the wall. 'I've missed your stories so much. Won't you tell me what happened to Rama and the princess?'

Sara nodded and smiled.

CHAPTER FIFTEEN

One morning in the very early spring, Hanuman, the Indian man's monkey, decided to go for a walk. He walked across the wooden plank that connected his master's window with Sara's.

Sara was tying up the laces in her shoes when the monkey pushed her shutter open. 'Hanuman!' she cried in surprise. 'What are you doing here?'

Hanuman climbed onto her shoulder and put its hands over her eyes. Sara giggled.

That day, Miss Minchin was leading the girls on their daily walk. As they marched in a crocodile along Fifth Avenue, Ermengarde told Betsy and Gertrude all about her visit to Sara in the attic. 'I can't go every evening, because Minchin might find out,' Ermengarde explained. 'I wait for Sara's signal, then I know it's safe.'

'Oh, how exciting!' Gertrude exclaimed.

'Does Sara understand about us not speaking to her?' Betsy wanted to know.

'Oh yes,' Ermengarde replied. 'She pretends Minchin put a spell on all of you to be silent. But I broke the spell because of my courage,' she added proudly.

Betsy sighed. 'We should make it up to her,' she said, looking fixedly at Miss Minchin. 'Think,' she told her friends. 'What's the worst thing Minchin ever did to her?'

'She took her locket away,' Gertrude suggested.

'That's it,' Ermengarde said, and her eyes began to glow. She had a plan.

The next day, Betsy tiptoed up to Miss Minchin's office door and peered through the keyhole; she was waiting for Miss Minchin to leave. At last, she saw Miss Minchin put on her coat. Amelia was sitting at her sister's desk, correcting the girls' Latin exercises.

When Miss Minchin opened her office door to leave, Betsy stood and smiled at her innocently. Miss Minchin gave her a sharp look and walked away along the hall.

Ermengarde was stationed by the front door. She smiled, too. 'Goodbye, Miss Minchin,' she said sweetly.

Miss Minchin nodded. She was beginning to look a little suspicious.

Ermengarde waited until she could see Miss Minchin walking away down the pavement, then she signalled to Betsy. Betsy peered through the keyhole again. Amelia had sat back in Miss Minchin's chair and now she was putting her feet up on Miss Minchin's desk.

Betsy nodded to Gertrude, who was at the bottom of the stairs. Gertrude turned, looked upstairs and nodded to Lottie.

At Gertrude's signal, Lottie took a deep breath and began one of her famous tantrums. 'Waahhh!!!' she wailed.

Becky came out of the kitchen just in time to see Amelia rushing upstairs to find out what was wrong with Lottie. Becky watched as Ermengarde, Betsy and Gertrude slipped into Miss Minchin's office. Then the three girls shut the door behind them.

'The locket has to be in here somewhere,' Betsy insisted as she began searching through Miss Minchin's desk.

Lottie continued to wail and shriek. Becky

was still standing near Miss Minchin's office door, not knowing what to do. She had not been let in on the secret of what was happening.

Out in the street, Miss Minchin realized that she had left one of her gloves behind on her desk, so she headed back to school at a rapid pace.

Miss Minchin could hear Lottie's tantrum even before she opened the front door.

She shook her head in disgust. 'Will you please get that child under control,' she snapped at Amelia. Then she stormed towards her office. Becky watched in horror as Miss Minchin reached her office door and turned the doorknob, flinging the door open.

Inside the office, Ermengarde had just found the locket in a drawer, and she held it up excitedly. At that very moment, the door was flung open. The three girls inside froze.

Becky thought quickly. Before Miss Minchin could enter her office, she screamed – very loudly.

Miss Minchin jumped back, away from her door, and glared at Becky. 'Well, what is it?' she asked coldly.

'I . . . I . . .' Becky struggled to find an excuse. The three girls smiled at her gratefully as they tiptoed out of Miss Minchin's office and away behind her back, closing the door behind them. Miss Minchin never noticed them; her eyes were still on Becky.

'I thought I saw a mouse,' Becky said finally. Miss Minchin sniffed disdainfully and turned round to go in to her office. She ran straight into her closed door.

CHAPTER SIXTEEN

Spring came slowly to New York, but it did come. The same day that Ermengarde found Sara's locket, Sara discovered a nest of baby birds under the school's front window.

She was just leaning towards the nest when she heard a noise coming from next door. Sara turned in time to see Ram Dass loading Mr Randolph's wheelchair into a waiting carriage. Then he climbed in beside his master.

'The young man they found may not be John,' Sara heard Ram Dass say.

'Of course he is,' Mr Randolph answered, and then ordered the driver to go to St Mary's Hospital. Sara watched the carriage drive away down the street.

'Sara, didn't I tell you to go to the market?'

Mabel said crossly, appearing on the front doorstep.

'Yes, ma'am,' Sara said, and she rushed away.

At St Mary's Hospital, Dr Reed was standing next to Mr Randolph. They were both staring at a man who lay, asleep, in a hospital bed. Layers of bandages covered the man's eyes. Ram Dass was standing in the doorway, watching his master.

'He's suffering from acute amnesia, one of the rare side-effects of poison gas,' the doctor told Mr Randolph. 'His eyes will heal in time. His memory, who can say?'

Mr Randolph stared sadly at the patient. 'He's not my son,' he said quietly.

The doctor looked discouraged. 'I'm sorry, Mr Randolph. He was found in severe shock, with no coat, no identification. We thought he might be John.'

Ram Dass walked towards his master and put his hand on the old man's shoulder. 'I'm sorry, sahib.'

Mr Randolph sadly wheeled his chair away.

Outside the hospital, Mr Randolph turned towards Ram Dass. 'You must think me a fool,' he said to his servant. 'A wise man would not have come.'

'That soldier needs to be cared for,' Ram Dass said.

'He's not my responsibility,' Mr Randolph replied.

'This soldier was in John's regiment. If his memory returns, he might tell sahib what happened to son,' Ram Dass reminded his master.

Mr Randolph began to look up and take an interest. Together, they began to make plans to bring the wounded soldier home.

Chapter Seventeen

That evening, Ermengarde, Betsy, Lottie and Gertrude were to be seen poking their heads out of their rooms. They all waited until Miss Minchin had turned out the lights and closed her bedroom door. Then they tiptoed in their nightgowns up to the attic door.

Becky was sitting on Sara's bed, holding her hands over Sara's eyes. 'What's happening?' Sara asked Becky as she heard footsteps on the attic stairs.

'It's a surprise,' Becky whispered excitedly.

Just then the door opened. Ermengarde led Betsy, Gertrude and Lottie into the room. Becky took her hands away so that Sara could see them.

'What are you doing here?' Sara asked.

'We brought you something,' Ermengarde said.

She glanced at the others. Betsy, Gertrude and Lottie had never been in Sara's room before and they were looking around in shock. Ermengarde coughed to get their attention.

The five girls, including Becky, lined up in front of Sara. 'Princess Sara, we would like to present you with something we rescued,' Ermengarde began.

'In a most daring adventure,' Betsy added.

Lottie stepped forward and presented the gold locket to Sara.

Tears filled Sara's eyes and for a few moments she could not think of anything to say. 'You are all the best friends anyone could ever ask for,' she said finally, giving them all a big hug.

Suddenly, a loud screech at the window made all the girls jump. Hanuman, the monkey, was perched on the sill outside Sara's window. Everyone except Sara and Becky screamed and dived under the bed.

'It's all right,' Sara assured them. They climbed back out and she introduced them to Hanuman.

'W-where did he come from?' Lottie asked.

'Right next door – look!' Becky said. She

pointed to the wooden plank that connected Sara's window to Ram Dass's.

'He comes to visit me all the time, don't you?' Sara asked the monkey.

'Can you really talk to him, Sara?' Betsy asked.

'Yes. Hanuman, say hello to my friends,' Sara said. Hanuman turned to the girls, bowed its head and squealed. The girls all giggled.

Hanuman perched on Sara's shoulder while she told the girls a story. They had all insisted that she tell them some more about Princess Sita and Prince Rama.

When Sara arrived at the part about the ten-headed monster, the monkey leapt off her shoulder and landed on Ermengarde's head. The girls all screamed in fright.

Miss Minchin poked her head out of her bedroom door: she thought she heard a noise upstairs.

The girls heard Miss Minchin's door creak open. No one dared say a word until they heard the door close once more.

'Maybe we'd better save the rest of the story for later,' Sara suggested. She picked Hanuman up and carried it to the window. The girls gathered around to say goodbye to the monkey.

At that moment, Miss Minchin entered Sara's attic room. '*What is going on here?!!!*' she asked sharply.

The girls spun around and cowered down at the sight of her; Miss Minchin had rarely looked so angry. Sara hid the locket in the palm of her hand. 'It's not their fault,' she said. 'I . . . I asked them to come.'

Miss Minchin clenched her jaw. She turned to her students first. 'You four, get downstairs immediately,' she said in an icy tone.

Ermengarde, Betsy, Gertrude and Lottie did not have to be told twice. They scampered quickly out through the door.

'Becky, you will remain, locked in your room, for the entire day tomorrow without meals,' Miss Minchin went on. '*Go!*'

After Becky had rushed away, Miss Minchin turned to Sara. 'And *you*,' she began, 'will perform all *her* chores in addition to your own. You will go without breakfast, lunch, or dinner.'

Sara stared at Miss Minchin but did not say anything. That only made the schoolmistress angrier.

'Sara Crewe, it is time you learned that real life has nothing to do with your little fantasy games,' Miss Minchin said. 'Do you understand me?'

'Yes, ma'am,' Sara answered.

Miss Minchin turned to go.

'But I don't believe what you said,' Sara added.

Miss Minchin slowly turned and faced Sara again. 'Don't tell me you still fancy yourself a princess,' she said with a sneer. 'My God, child, look in a mirror.'

Sara continued to stare steadily at Miss Minchin. 'I am a princess,' she said firmly. 'All girls are. Even if they live in tiny old attics. Even if they dress in rags. Even if they aren't beautiful, or young, or smart. They're still princesses.' Sara paused. 'Didn't your father ever tell you that?' she asked.

Miss Minchin stared at her, speechless. No, no one had ever said that to her; no one had ever loved her, or even told her that they loved her. But she did not tell this to Sara. Instead, she only became angrier.

'If I find you up here with any of the other girls again, I'll throw you out into the street,' she warned Sara. Then she stormed out of the room.

CHAPTER EIGHTEEN

After Miss Minchin had left, Sara sat on her cot and opened her locket. She smiled sadly at her mother's picture.

Becky came through the opening in the wall and sat down next to her.

'What are we going to do?' Becky asked her sadly. 'A whole day with nothing to eat.' Becky's stomach rumbled. She was so hungry that she began to cry.

Sara put her arms round her friend.

'I'm scared,' Becky told her. 'If Minchin throws me out, I got no place to go. No family . . . nobody wanting me.'

'That's not true,' Sara replied. 'I'm here with you. I've always thought of us as sisters.'

'You have?' Becky sounded surprised.

'Of course,' Sara answered. 'Why don't we make a promise right now to always look out for each other. No matter what happens, we'll never be alone.'

'It's a promise,' Becky said, and she hugged Sara.

'Now,' Sara said. 'What are we going to do about food?'

'Starve, I guess,' Becky answered her.

'No,' Sara said, shaking her head. 'We'll eat a great feast before we go to sleep.'

'Feast?' Becky asked, looking around in the small room. 'What feast?'

'Don't you see that table over there?' Sara said. She gestured towards her rickety crate. 'It's covered with a beautiful cloth and candles. And trays and trays of good things to eat.'

'But . . . I don't see any food,' Becky insisted.

'Try, Becky. Just make believe,' Sara almost pleaded.

Becky looked at the crate and thought for a moment. 'Muffins,' she said finally.

'Good!' Sara said. 'What kind?'

'Every kind of muffin God ever made. And all of them hot!'

Sara looked pleased. 'Mmm, smell those sausages,' she said as she pretended to lift a lid off the tray.

'Oh, I love sausages,' Becky said.

Sara and Becky went on talking well into the night about what they would eat, and what they would wear to their elegant banquet.

In the house next door, Ram Dass stroked Hanuman and watched the girls from his window. He could hear their conversation, and it touched him. It also gave him an idea . . .

The following morning, Hanuman tried very hard to wake Sara by tickling her face. Sara stirred sleepily. She felt a thick, silk quilt over her and the warm glow of a real fire in her fireplace. She closed her eyes, smiling. What a wonderful dream this was.

Hanuman squealed and ran away. This time Sara woke up. She looked around, stunned.

Her room had been transformed. A fire crackled merrily in the grate. A plush rug covered the floor. Silk fabric draped the walls, and flowers filled the room. A pretty tablecloth covered the old crate, and on it sat trays of food and two sets of plates, knives and forks.

Sara looked down at her bed. Becky still lay there, asleep, next to her. A thick down quilt

73

covered the bed, at the foot of which were two pairs of slippers and two beautiful robes.

When Becky woke up, she gasped when she looked round her at the room. 'I think maybe you went a little too far this time,' Becky said. She sounded scared.

'It wasn't me,' Sara answered her.

Becky and Sara slipped on their new robes and slippers. 'I feel like I've been touched by an angel,' Becky said in wonder.

Sara lifted the lid off a plate of sausages. 'Look, just what we ordered,' she said.

'I'm a little scared about all this,' Becky said.

'Me too,' Sara said, nodding. 'Do you think we shouldn't eat it?'

'I ain't *that* scared,' Becky said.

The two girls laughed and helped themselves to the delicious food.

CHAPTER NINETEEN

That morning, the wounded soldier from the hospital was eating breakfast in Ram Dass's room. The plate he was eating from matched the china that Sara and Becky were using next door. However, his eyes were still covered by bandages.

'I will help you,' Ram Dass told the soldier as he placed a warm muffin in his hand.

'Thank you for all your kindness,' the soldier said.

'It is nothing, sahib,' Ram Dass replied.

The soldier sat up at the sound of the word 'sahib'. 'That word,' he said. 'It sounds so familiar – and yet I don't know what it means.'

'It is not English,' Ram Dass said. 'We use it where I am from – in India.'

'India,' the soldier said softly.

'You know it?' Ram Dass asked him.

The soldier tried to remember. 'No,' he answered finally. 'Everything's a blur. Maybe, someday, I'll sort it out.'

'You will, sahib,' Ram Dass said kindly.

That evening, a full moon was hanging in the sky. Sara leant out of her window, watching as Amelia lowered a heavy suitcase to the ground. Francis, the milkman, was waiting outside to catch it.

To Sara's great surprise, Amelia then hauled herself through the window. Soon the two were driving away together in Francis' milk cart. Amelia and Francis had eloped.

Now she thought about it, Sara was not surprised. She knew that Amelia and the milkman liked each other; they often talked together in the kitchen. And Amelia had never seemed very happy at school, with Miss Minchin always bossing her about. Sara leant further out of the window, lost in thought.

Suddenly Sara heard the angry voice of Miss Minchin behind her. 'Where is it?' Miss Minchin demanded. 'Where is the locket?'

Sara whirled around. She touched the locket round her neck.

'Give it to me!' Miss Minchin said and she advanced towards Sara. Tearfully, Sara removed the locket. Miss Minchin snatched it from her. Then she realized with a shock that Sara's room had somehow miraculously changed.

'What is all this?' she asked Sara. 'Where did it come from?'

'I ... I don't know,' Sara replied. 'I just woke up, and it was here.'

'You stole all of it, didn't you? Just like you stole this locket!'

'No!' Sara protested.

Miss Minchin narrowed her small eyes. 'You're nothing but a dirty little thief,' she said.

'Miss Minchin —' Sara pleaded.

'Pack your things,' Miss Minchin interrupted her. 'You'll be leaving with the police, very shortly.'

Sara was too terrified to say any more.

Miss Minchin left the room, slamming the door behind her.

Sara banged on her door, but Miss Minchin had locked her in. 'Please!' she said, sobbing. 'I didn't do it!'

Downstairs, Miss Minchin called the police. 'You heard me. I want her picked up immediately,' she said into the phone. She glanced at

Sara's locket, then threw it angrily against the wall. It burst open . . .

Clouds began to cover the full moon. The wind gusted and thunder rumbled overhead. Rain pelted down against the windows.

Sara lay down on her bed and cried and cried.

Becky tried to comfort her. 'I'm sure they'll believe you,' Becky said.

'No.' Sara's voice sounded muffled. 'I have to get away.'

'But how?' Becky asked. 'My room's locked, too.'

Just then the girls heard a van pull up in front of the school. 'The police, they're here!' Becky said from the window.

Sara looked outside. Her heart sank when she saw that the wooden plank connecting her room with the house next door was missing.

Quickly, Sara took one of the wooden boards from under her mattress. With Becky's help, she laid the plank on her windowsill. It stretched across to Ram Dass's.

Miss Minchin ushered the two policemen inside and led them up the attic stairs.

Sara climbed out of the window on to the unsteady board. The rain poured down, making the wood slippery.

'Sara, you'll fall!' Becky warned.

'I can do it,' Sara said. She turned to give Becky one last hug. 'I'll come back for you,' she promised.

Sara began her walk across the board while Hanuman watched her. At that moment, Miss Minchin burst into Sara's room with the two policemen. She saw Becky by the open window and she leant out.

'What are you doing?' she called to Sara. 'Come back here this instant!' She reached out to grab the hem of Sara's dress. Sara stumbled – and almost fell off – the slippery board. However, she regained her balance and began to crawl.

Miss Minchin lost her temper. 'The little beast is running away!' she shouted.

Suddenly a clap of thunder shook the building. A gutter fell from the roof and hit the board, snapping it in half.

'Sara!' Becky screamed.

Sara managed to clutch on to Ram Dass's windowsill, where she dangled by her fingertips above the alley, far below. Becky, Miss Minchin and the policemen watched in horror.

Sara took a deep breath. Carefully, she managed to pull herself slowly up. Hanuman waited for her to climb inside before it jumped into her arms.

'Well, don't just stand there,' Miss Minchin told the policemen angrily. 'Go next door and find her!'

Chapter Twenty

Sara could not believe she was really in Mr Randolph's house, but she wasn't safe yet. She made her way quietly down the big staircase, with Hanuman following her.

On the ground floor of the brownstone house, Sara heard muffled voices coming from the study.

Mr Randolph was sitting by the fire, chatting with the wounded soldier. The younger man no longer had bandages on his eyes; he could see now.

'It's just the not knowing that's so painful,' Mr Randolph said. 'I can't let go of John until I find out what happened.'

'I'm sorry. I wish I could help you,' the soldier replied.

Sara tiptoed past the open door of the study. Hanuman walked silently behind her. The two men did not notice.

'You sound as though you've experienced such a loss,' Mr Randolph continued.

The wounded soldier nodded. 'It's strange – feeling your heart remember something your mind cannot,' he said.

By now Sara was at the front door. She reached for the knob just as Miss Minchin and the two policemen banged on the door from outside.

Sara dashed into the living-room, closing the sliding doors behind her.

'Who can that be at this hour!' Mr Randolph wondered.

Ram Dass left the study to go and answer the door.

'I'm sorry to bother you, but a child from the school has escaped into your house,' Miss Minchin told Ram Dass.

'Ram Dass, what is going on here?' Mr Randolph asked as he wheeled his chair into the front hall.

'There is a child hiding in this house unlawfully,' Miss Minchin replied for him.

'What?' Mr Randolph exclaimed.

The policemen then took charge. One policeman searched the upstairs while the other made straight for the living-room door.

Sara heard the policeman's heavy footsteps approaching. Quickly, she opened another set of sliding doors that connected the living-room with the study. If Sara had had time, and if she had not been so scared, she would have marvelled at what a wonderful house this was.

Suddenly a bolt of lightning came down and struck the house, leaving it in complete darkness.

'What now?!' Mr Randolph exclaimed. 'Ram Dass, bring some candles!'

As the policeman entered the living-room, Sara tiptoed into the study. The wounded soldier was sitting there, in the shadows. He heard Sara come in, but he could not see her.

'Who's there?' he called out.

Sara had not been expecting there to be anyone in the study; she was so scared, she fell to the floor and began to cry.

'I won't hurt you,' the wounded soldier said as he got up and walked towards Sara. 'Won't you tell me your name?'

The room was so dark, Sara couldn't see the soldier's face. 'Sara,' she answered, with a slight whimper in her voice.

'Sara,' the wounded soldier repeated. 'That's such a pretty name,' and he stepped into the light cast by the fire in the fireplace.

For the first time, Sara saw the soldier's face. She stared and stared as if she was looking at a ghost. Slowly, she got up off the floor.

'Da . . . Daddy . . .' she said.

'What . . .? What did you say?' Captain Crewe murmured.

Sara threw her arms around his legs and hugged him. 'Daddy,' she repeated. 'Daddy, it's me . . . it's Sara!'

Captain Crewe looked bewildered. He knelt in front of the little girl. 'Sara, do you know me?' he asked.

'Oh God, Daddy, don't you remember me?' Sara sounded heartbroken.

She heard the sound of footsteps and voices outside the room.

'Daddy, please! You must know me!' she sobbed. '*It's Sara!* Remember?! Remember India!? And Maya? And mean Clara Pideson?'

Captain Crewe tried. 'I can't seem to remember,' he said, shaking his head.

At that moment, Miss Minchin and the policemen burst into the room. Mr Randolph wheeled himself in, followed by Ram Dass.

'Sara!' Miss Minchin exclaimed.

'Daddy, please!' Sara pleaded. Miss Minchin turned and gazed at the wounded soldier. She recognized Captain Crewe at once, and she went very pale.

'Do you know this man?' Mr Randolph asked Sara.

'Daddy, tell them!'

Miss Minchin noticed Captain Crewe's blank look. Without hesitation, she turned to the police. 'This child has no father,' she announced. 'Take her away.'

'No, no,' Sara sobbed.

Captain Crewe looked on helplessly as the police began to drag Sara out of the room.

Ram Dass was watching Captain Crewe's face intently. Then, very slowly, he began to hum the Indian folksong.

'Daddy, do you hear that? It's the song,' Sara said, struggling to break free. She too began to sing the words to the song, while the police were pulling her out of the room and Miss Minchin and Mr Randolph followed.

Ram Dass stayed where he was, humming softly. His eyes never left the captain's face. All at once, Captain Crewe began singing the last part of the song to himself. The words came flooding back to him – and, with them, so did his memory.

'Sara!' he called. He remembered!

Chapter Twenty-One

Captain Crewe rushed outside. Miss Minchin and the police were leading Sara to the waiting police van. Sara was still struggling to free herself and crying as if her heart was breaking.

'Sara!' Captain Crewe cried as he raced towards the van.

Sara broke free and rushed into her father's arms.

'Oh, my darling. My darling Sara,' her father said, kissing her.

'Oh, Daddy, you're back. You're back!' Sara shouted.

Miss Minchin stood in the background and watched the scene; she looked furious. When at last she turned away, she saw the policemen looking at her with raised eyebrows. She knew she was in trouble for lying.

*

Two months later, many things had changed. Miss Minchin's Seminary was now called The Randolph School for Girls. Miss Minchin had been allowed to stay on, on condition that she agreed to do a different job at the school, so now she worked there as a chimney sweep.

Mr Randolph sat outside in his wheelchair, watching the schoolgirls playing a game with a ball in the park. Ram Dass and Hanuman were near him.

A carriage pulled up at the kerb. Captain Crewe stepped out and held the door open for Sara and Becky to climb down. All three were beautifully dressed.

'All ready for your trip?' Mr Randolph greeted them.

Captain Crewe nodded. 'I can't thank you enough, Mr Randolph, for everything you've done. Your loan was very generous.'

Mr Randolph smiled warmly. 'No more generous than what you tried to do for my son,' he said.

Captain Crewe gave the elderly man a sympathetic look.

'Keep the money as long as you need it,' Mr Randolph continued. 'Starting over is never easy.'

'No sir,' Captain Crewe answered. 'But it sure feels good to be going back to India.'

Ram Dass smiled at him.

Ermengarde, Betsy, Gertrude and Lottie left the game to say goodbye to Sara and Becky. Sara handed Ermengarde a book, wrapped up with a bow.

'The Rama . . . naya,' Lottie tried to read the title over Ermengarde's shoulder.

'Ramayana,' Sara corrected her gently. 'The greatest of Indian legends. It's the whole story I told you, start to finish.'

'Oh,' Ermengarde said. 'It'll be like you're really here with us!'

Many weeks later, Captain Crewe, Sara and Becky stood on the deck of the ship. In the distance they could see the Himalayas welcoming them with open arms.